The Legend of the
Cape May Diamond

By Trinka Hakes Noble *and Illustrated by* E.B. Lewis

For Denise Brunkus—
A true friend and precious Cape May diamond.

T.H.N.

✦

To the Lenape tribe—past, present, and future.

E.B.L.

Text Copyright © 2007 Trinka Hakes Noble
Illustration Copyright © 2007 E.B. Lewis

Sleeping Bear Press™

315 E. Eisenhower Parkway, Ste. 200
Ann Arbor, MI 48108
www.sleepingbearpress.com

© 2007 Sleeping Bear Press is an imprint of Gale,
a part of Cengage Learning.

10 9 8 7 6 5 4 3 2

Library of Congress Cataloging-in-Publication Data

Noble, Trinka Hakes.
The legend of the Cape May diamond / written by Trinka Hakes Noble;
illustrated by E.B. Lewis.
p. cm.
Summary: For thousands of years, quartz fragments have traveled down the
Delaware River (once called the Wehittck by the Lenape Indians), washing ashore
near a place settled by the Dutch explorer Cornelius Jacobson Mey, where they
are gathered as treasures and known as Cape May Diamonds.
ISBN 13: 978-1-58536-279-0
[1. Cape May diamonds—Fiction. 2. Indians of North America—Fiction.
3. Delaware Indians—Fiction. 4. Delaware River (N.Y.-Del. and N.J.)—Fiction.]
I. Lewis, Earl B., ill. II. Title.
PZ7.N6715Lem 2007
[E]—dc22   2006026581
Printed by China Translation & Printing Services Limited, Guangdong Province, China. 2nd printing.   11/2009

About the Legend of the Cape May Diamond

Some legends are lost forever in the sands of time. Other legends are hidden for ages and never found. For thousands of years the legend of the Cape May diamond lay locked in the mysterious glow of small pebbles hidden beneath the waters of the old Delaware River. It takes two thousand years for these small pebbles to complete their travel downriver to the Delaware Bay. But even a journey lasting two millennia must one day find its destination. And so, with the passing of time and tides, these small stones and their ancient story would be cast into the glistening sunlight on the shores of Cape May for all to see.

—*Trinka Hakes Noble*

In a time long past, when the Delaware River was called the *Wehittck*, its bountiful waters flowed through the heart of an ancient land called *Lenapehoking*. For twelve thousand years Lenapehoking was the ancestral homeland of the *Lenape* people, the "common people." They spoke a common language called *Algonquin* and lived peacefully in many tribal villages along the banks of their beloved river.

But it was high in the old Appalachian
Mountains where the Delaware River was formed
by melting glaciers that the legendary story of the
Cape May diamond begins.

Here the young Delaware rushed and tumbled along, full of
energy and promise. But the young river could not tell where it
was going. From its high vantage point it could not see beyond
the many twists and turns, hills and bends.

"I will send my best daughters downstream to see where my
journey leads," said the river with great hope. "Someday they
will return to tell me what they have seen."

So, with its swift currents, the young river began to erode pieces of pure quartz crystal from rich veins in the mountainsides, sending these small stones, these little daughters of the Delaware, on their way.

Like dutiful daughters the little stones did as the river asked. For thousands of years they journeyed along the river bottom, unseen. Over and over again the little stones were naturally scoured and burnished and polished by the rough riverbed, then washed clean by the slow-moving currents until they began to shine like gems.

It was as though the river had turned the little stones into sparkling eyes, bright and clear, so they could see everything.

To the north and west, the small stones saw how the river watered the vast forests of Lenapehoking that rose high into the mountains on either side. From these forests the Lenape built bark-covered lodges to shield them from the cold winter winds. From large tree trunks they crafted dugout canoes for travel and trade up and down the Delaware. The rest was used for wooden bowls and splint baskets, spears and tools, cooking and warmth. Nothing was wasted.

The little stones nodded their approval. "This will please the river."

To the east the mountains gave way to densely wooded foothills filled with black bear, deer, and wild game. Generations of woodland animals came to drink as the little stones looked on. Again the Lenape hunters took only what they needed for their people, and with respect, gave thanks to the animals' spirit.

"This will please the river," nodded the little stones.

Further downriver, in early spring the little stones observed the running of the shad, salmon, and herring as they traveled upstream to their spawning grounds. With nets, weirs, and spears, the Lenape caught and dried only what they needed to replenish their winter food supplies so their people would not go hungry.

Again the little stones nodded, "This will please the river."

As the river moved south through the heart of Lenapehoking,
it slowed and widened, nourishing fertile plains where in summer
the Lenape cultivated lush gardens, growing maize, beans, squash,
pumpkins, and sunflowers. In the fall they gathered their crops
and hung them to dry in the warm autumn sun.

Once more the little stones nodded, "This will please the river."

Now the river had widened even more where the plains of Lenapehoking rolled gently down to the great salt ocean. Here, on sandy white beaches, bands of Lenape would gather in summer to collect shellfish, mussels, and clams. From the inside of clamshells they made purple and silvery-white beads called *wampum*, which they used for currency and trade.

The Lenape of the south, the *Unami*, or the "downriver people," generously traded with the Lenape of the north, the *Munsee*, or "people from *Minisink*, the stony place." Everyone benefited.

Still again the little stones nodded, "This will please the river."

But then something changed.

The little stones were cast into a great wide bay. The water became murky, harsh, and salty. Powerful tides from the great salt ocean began to push and pull the little stones rapidly toward the mouth of the bay.

The little daughters of the Delaware resisted because they did not want to leave their river and be swept out to sea, never to be seen again.

But Lenapehoking had a narrow peninsula of land, like a long finger, which jutted out into the mouth of the bay. It caught the little daughters and gently tossed them upon its shores before they were lost forever. In the shallow waves of the bay, the sunlight touched the little stones and they began to glisten like tears in the wet sand.

It was as though these shining bright eyes of the river had turned to salty tears because they never would get back to tell the Delaware River of its long and beautiful journey.

But all was not lost.

It just so happened that a band of Lenape called the *Kechemeche* lived on this very peninsula of land and, like many summers before, they were out gathering shellfish along the sandy shore.

No one knows for sure who was the first person to find one of these precious daughters of the Delaware, glistening like teardrops in the sand. Perhaps it was a young Kechemeche boy named *Ma-eh-hu-mund*, One-Who-Gathers-Things.

True to his name, One-Who-Gathers-Things would have been combing the beach for hours, collecting pretty stones and shells to add to his deerskin pouch. Children were prized by the Lenape and allowed to play and explore freely. But even One-Who-Gathers-Things would have known that this precious stone was sacred because Lenape children were taught by their elders that all things had living spirits, called *manetuwak*, even a stone.

With great excitement, One-Who-Gathers-Things would have raced to the *Sachem*, the tribe's wise chief and leader, with this rare stone clutched in his hand.

When the Sachem held up this translucent stone to the sun, it was so clear that he could see right through it. To be able to see through a stone gave it great meaning and power, so the wise Sachem proclaimed this precious stone would never be used for wampum but would have a higher purpose.

And so the Lenape people made this sacred stone the symbol of loyalty and lasting friendship, because a true friend is a trusted friend with nothing to hide, just like this rare translucent stone.

Over the centuries the largest of these sacred stones were exchanged to seal the bonds of loyalty and friendship among the many Lenape tribes up and down the Delaware River.

But things would soon change in Lenapehoking.

In 1621 a Dutch explorer named Cornelius Jacobsen Mey sailed into the bay and named the peninsula Cape Mey and the narrow tip Cape Mey Point. Other European settlers followed, including the Dutch, the Swedes, and lastly, the English, who altered the spelling to Cape May.

The Lenape called these European settlers *shuwunnock*, the "salty people," because they came from the great salt ocean and were white as sea foam. The Europeans called the Lenape the "river people," and when the English named the Delaware River after the first colonial governor of Virginia, Sir Thomas West, Lord de la Warre, the Lenape became known as the Delaware, too.

One of the last known exchanges of this sacred stone between the Lenape happened in 1735. At a great council, the Kechemeche tribe decided to move further inland, away from the European settlers, but their chief, King Nummy, stayed behind.

Before they left, the Kechemeche tribe presented King Nummy with a large flawless stone to pledge their enduring loyalty and friendship to him.

In the old whaling days of New Jersey, King Nummy presented this stone to an early settler, Christopher Leaming, to seal their friendship. Leaming had the stone sent to Amsterdam where it was polished, cut, and faceted into a diamond.

And so this sacred stone of the Lenape became known as the Cape May diamond.

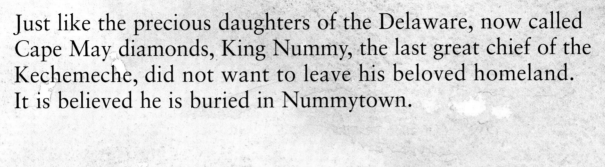

Just like the precious daughters of the Delaware, now called
Cape May diamonds, King Nummy, the last great chief of the
Kechemeche, did not want to leave his beloved homeland.
It is believed he is buried in Nummytown.

Cape May continued to flourish, becoming a popular seaside resort. It was referred to as the summer White House as many early presidents spent their summers there. In the 1860s the little town of Cape May became a seaside gem with its many beautiful Victorian summer homes and picturesque lighthouse on Cape May Point.

It was in this Victorian era that the Cape May diamond became very popular. Many summer visitors combed the beaches for hours searching for these precious little stones.

To this very day the Delaware River is sending these little stones on their long journey to Cape May. So you can still find Cape May diamonds along Delaware Bay beaches, glistening like tears in the shallow waves because they never got back to tell the river of its beautiful journey.

But when a Cape May diamond is given as a gift to seal the lasting bonds of true friendship, these little sparkling daughters of the Delaware will still be nodding their approval.

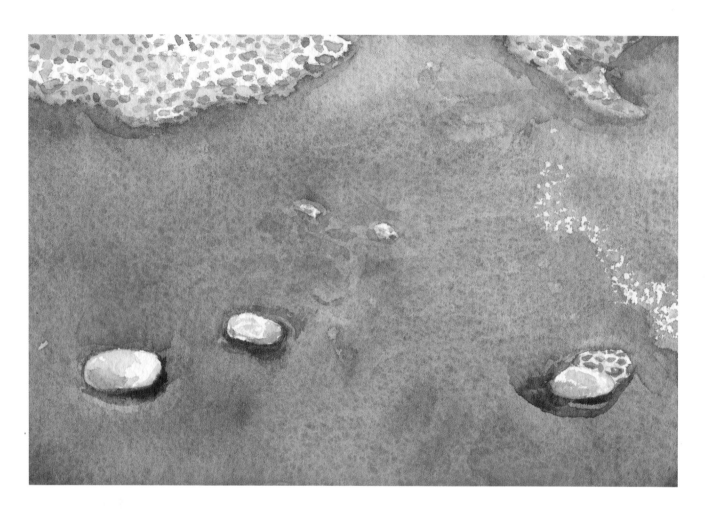

"This will please the river."